The HAUNTED LIBRARY

FOR THE REAL

MARGARET
AND HENRY

—DHB

* * * * * * * * * * * * * * *

GROSSET & DUNLAP
Penguin Young Readers Group
An Imprint of Penguin Random House LLC

Text copyright © 2016 by Dori Hillestad Butler. Illustrations copyright © 2016 by Aurore Damant. All rights reserved. Published by Grosset & Dunlap, an imprint of Penguin Random House LLC, 345 Hudson Street, New York, New York 10014. GROSSET & DUNLAP is a trademark of Penguin Random House LLC. Printed in the USA.

Library of Congress Cataloging-in-Publication Data is available.

ISBN 978-0-448-48940-7 (pbk)   10 9 8 7 6 5 4 3 2 1
ISBN 978-0-448-48941-4 (hc)   10 9 8 7 6 5 4 3 2 1

The HAUNTED LIBRARY
THE GHOST IN THE TREE HOUSE

BY DORI HILLESTAD BUTLER
ILLUSTRATED BY AURORE DAMANT

GROSSET & DUNLAP ★ AN IMPRINT OF PENGUIN RANDOM HOUSE

GHOSTLY GLOSSARY

EXPAND
When ghosts make themselves larger

GLOW
What ghosts do so humans can see them

HAUNT
Where ghosts live

PASS THROUGH
When ghosts travel through walls, doors, and other solid objects

SHRINK
When ghosts make themselves smaller

SKIZZY
When ghosts feel sick to their stomachs

SOLIDS
What ghosts call humans

SPEW
Ghostly vomit

SWIM
When ghosts move freely through the air

TRANSFORMATION
When a ghost takes a solid object and turns it into a ghostly object

WAIL
What ghosts do so humans can hear them

CHAPTER 1

SECRET CLUB

Who left the TV on in here again?"
Mr. Kendall grumbled as he
wandered into the living room. He
picked up the remote and turned
off the TV.

"Hey!" Little John cried as he hovered
above the couch. "We were watching
that!"

"He can't hear you," Kaz reminded his
brother.

"Oh yeah," Little John said.

Kaz and Little John were ghosts. They used to live in an old abandoned schoolhouse with the rest of their ghost family. But when the schoolhouse was torn down, the family got separated. Now Kaz and Little John lived in the library with their solid friend Claire and *her* family.

Claire could see ghosts when they weren't glowing, and she could hear ghosts when they weren't wailing. Her dad, Mr. Kendall, could not.

Little John swam over. His whole body glowed. "We . . . were . . . watching . . . that," he wailed loudly in Mr. Kendall's face.

Claire's dad jumped. He could see and hear Little John now. "Sorry," he said, backing away. "I . . . uh . . . forgot we were sharing our home with a bunch of ghosts."

"Not . . . a . . . *bunch* . . . of . . . ghosts," Little John wailed. "Just . . . three."

Beckett was the third ghost. He wasn't related to Kaz and Little John, but he'd been at the library way longer than they had. Beckett preferred books to TV, so he was probably downstairs reading.

Claire's dad turned the TV back on and started to leave.

"You . . . can . . . watch . . . TV . . . with . . . us . . . if . . . you . . . want," Kaz wailed. He had only learned to wail a couple of weeks ago. He still couldn't glow.

"Oh, I don't think so," Claire's dad said. He couldn't see Kaz, so he talked to the air a few feet to the right of Kaz.

"Awww . . . come . . . on! . . . Stay . . . and . . . watch . . . with . . . us," Little John wailed. "It's . . . a . . . good . . . show."

"No. No, thank you," Claire's dad said

as he checked his watch. "Claire will be home soon. She may even be home now. Maybe she'll watch TV with you." He hurried away.

Little John's glow went out. "Why doesn't Claire's dad like us?" he asked Kaz.

"I don't think he *dis*likes us," Kaz replied.

"He doesn't like to be around us," Little John said. "He always leaves whenever he knows we're in the room."

Kaz had noticed that, too. "I think he feels weird around us."

"Why?" Little John asked.

"Because we're ghosts. And he's a solid," Kaz said.

"So?" Little John shrugged.

"So, we can see him, but he can't see us. That must feel weird. Remember, he didn't even know ghosts existed until

Claire and her mom and her grandma told him about us," Kaz said.

When Claire's mom and Grandma Karen were Claire's age, they could see and hear ghosts, too—just like Claire. But they couldn't do it anymore.

Claire and her mom and Grandma Karen had told Claire's dad about their unusual abilities a couple of weeks ago. It was hard for him to understand.

"Is he scared of us?" Little John asked.

Claire walked into the room. "Is who scared of you?" she asked, her green detective bag swinging back and forth at her side.

"Claire! You're home." Kaz swam over to greet her.

"Yup," Claire said. She turned to Little John. "Is who scared of you?" she asked again.

"Your dad," Little John said. "He always leaves when he knows we're around. I don't think he likes us."

"He likes you. He . . . just isn't used to ghosts," Claire said. "But don't worry, he'll get used to you . . . eventually. In the meantime, guess what, Kaz. We've got a new case!"

"We do?" Kaz said. "Tell me!"

He and Claire had formed a detective agency a few months ago. They called themselves C & K Ghost Detectives because they solved ghostly mysteries. So far, none of those cases had involved any real ghosts. There was always another explanation for whatever was going on. But Kaz kept hoping one of these cases would lead to the rest of his missing family.

"Well," Claire began, "there are these girls at my school—Margaret, Kenya, and Olivia. They're fourth-graders, too. They have a club that meets in a tree house in the woods behind their houses, but they think the tree house is haunted."

"Why do they think that?" Kaz asked.

"Because some strange things have been happening," Claire said. "Yesterday, the door slammed shut all by itself.

And they heard a ghostly voice warning them to 'Go awaaaaay!'" Claire tried to make her voice sound like a ghostly wail, but Kaz and Little John didn't think she sounded much like a ghost.

"Then last night," Claire went on, "right before Margaret went to bed, she looked out her bedroom window and she *saw* a ghost moving around inside the tree house. She said it was sort of bluish—"

"Like it was glowing?" Little John asked.

"If it was a ghost, it would have to be glowing for Margaret to see it," Kaz pointed out.

"Not if she's like Claire and can see ghosts," Little John said.

"I don't think she can," Claire said. "I told the girls I had to go home and get the rest of my ghost-hunting equipment,

13

but then I would come back and check out the tree house. Do you want to come with me?"

"Sure," Kaz said.

"Me too! Me too!" Little John cried.

Claire pulled her water bottle out of her bag, and the ghosts shrank down . . . down . . . down . . . and swam inside.

"Mom? Dad? Grandma?" Claire called as she looped the strap of the water bottle over her shoulder and headed for the stairs. "Kaz and I have a case. We'll be back in time for dinner."

Mom poked her head out of her office. "Okay, honey," she said. "Have fun."

* * * * * * * * * * * * * * *

There were lots of kids playing outside on Margaret's street. Claire, Kaz, and

Little John passed two girls on bikes, a boy and a girl tossing a Frisbee, and a group of boys and girls playing basketball. Up ahead they saw three girls sitting in a circle on the grass in front of a brown house.

"Those are our clients," Claire said in a low voice. She raised her bottle so Kaz and Little John could see the girls better. "The girl with the jacket is Margaret. The girl with the curly hair is Kenya. And the girl with the braids is Olivia."

Kaz thought he remembered Kenya from the play Claire had been in a couple of months ago. But he didn't think he'd ever seen Margaret or Olivia before.

"Hi, Claire!" All three girls hopped to their feet as Claire walked over.

Kaz saw a group of boys sitting hunched over a phone next door. A younger boy stood nearby, straining to see what they were doing.

"Do you have your ghost-hunting stuff?" Margaret asked Claire.

Claire held up her bag. "In here."

Kenya folded her arms across her chest. "I still don't think there's a ghost in the tree house," she said. "It's got to be something else."

"Like what?" Claire asked. She pulled a notebook and pencil out of her jacket pocket.

"Like maybe those boys over there." Kenya nodded toward the boys. "They've got a club, too. Maybe they're trying to scare us so they can have the tree house for *their* club."

"Maybe. But I *saw* the ghost!" Margaret said. She turned to Claire. "It was all floaty, and it sort of bobbed up and down in front of the tree house window."

"What do you think, Olivia?" Claire asked the third girl as she wrote down what Margaret said. "Do you think there's a ghost in the tree house?"

Olivia shrugged.

"Go away, Henry!" one of the big boys next door shouted suddenly at the younger boy.

"Yeah, quit spying on us. You're too little to be in our club!" said one of the other boys.

Henry came running over to the girls. "They won't let me join their club," he said.

Margaret glared at the boys. "Oh, you don't want to be in their club, anyway," she said, putting an arm around the younger boy. "They probably don't do anything fun."

"Yes, they do." Henry sniffed. "They hunt for treasure. They're letting Sam be in their club if he finds the treasure.

But they won't let me. Sam is only a year older than I am."

"That isn't very nice," Margaret said, glaring at the neighbor boys.

"Maybe I could be in your club instead," Henry said.

"Well . . . ," Margaret said, glancing at the other girls.

"Sorry," Kenya spoke up. "We're a girls' club. And you're a boy."

"Then you aren't nice, either," Henry said. He ran toward the brown house.

Margaret sighed. "Great. Now he'll probably tell on us." She barely got the sentence out before the front door opened at the brown house.

A lady with dark curly hair stepped out onto the porch. "Girls!" she called sternly. "Come here. I want to talk to you."

Margaret sighed. "I knew it," she said.

CHAPTER 2

SURPRISE!

Margaret!" the lady on the porch called again. "Now!"

"We'll see you later, Margaret," Kenya said as she and Olivia started to walk away.

"No, girls. I'd like to talk to *all* of you," the lady said, her arms folded across her chest.

"Uh-oh. Is Claire in trouble?" Little John asked from inside the water bottle.

"I don't know," Kaz said.

Claire shifted the water bottle on her shoulder and followed the other girls into the brown house.

The lady glanced curiously at Claire. "What's your name?" she asked as she closed the front door behind them. "I don't think I've seen you before."

"That's Claire, Mom," Margaret said. "She's here to help us catch the ghost in the tree house."

"I see," Margaret's mom said with a funny smile.

"Why is that lady smiling?" Little John asked.

"She probably doesn't believe in ghosts," Kaz told his brother. Lots of grown-up solids didn't. It was weird.

"We can *show* her ghosts are real!" Little John said. He passed through the bottle and expanded in front of Margaret's mom.

"No!" Kaz shouted. Before Little John could start to glow, Kaz charged through the bottle, grabbed his little brother around the waist, and swam with him behind the couch.

"We don't need to let them know we're here. Or that we're real," Kaz said. "Let's just listen for now."

"Okaaaay," Little John said.

The ghosts floated behind the couch.

"You girls know how I feel about secret clubs," Margaret's mom said.

Henry leaned against the doorjamb and chewed on his thumb.

"It's not a *secret* club," Margaret told her mom. "It's just a club."

"For girls," Kenya added.

Margaret's mom shook her head. "We're all friends in this neighborhood. Girls and boys can be in clubs together."

"Fine," Margaret said, slumping back against the wall. "Henry, do you want to join our club?"

Kenya's eyebrows shot up. Olivia's mouth dropped open.

"No." Henry shook his head. "I just don't want you to say I *can't* join it." He ran across the room and charged up the stairs. He was happy now.

The girls looked relieved.

"Well, I'm glad that's settled," Margaret's mom said. "Come into the kitchen and I'll make you girls a snack."

"What about the tree house?" Little John asked. "When do we get to see the ghost in the tree house?"

"Probably after they eat their snack," Kaz said as they followed Claire and the other girls.

Little John groaned. "Solids are *always* eating. I bet they can't even go one whole day without eating something."

"Little John?" came a voice from behind them. It was a man's voice. "Kaz? Is that you?"

Kaz, Little John, and even Claire whirled around.

"POPS!" Kaz and Little John cried out when they saw the ghost man.

They all flew into one another's arms.

"I thought I heard voices I recognized," Pops said as he hugged his boys.

"Where have you been?" Little John asked Pops.

"Where have *you* been?" Pops asked. The smile disappeared from his face as he looked beyond Kaz and Little John. "Why is that solid girl standing there with her mouth open? She's staring right at us."

"That's because she can see us," Kaz said. He swam over to Claire and floated beside her. Margaret, Kenya, and Olivia were already in the kitchen. "Pops, this is my friend Claire."

"Hi, Kaz's dad," Claire said softly. She gave a little wave.

"Your friend?" Pops snorted. "This solid girl is your *friend*? And what do you mean she can see us? We're not glowing."

"I know. But she can still see us," Kaz said.

"She's nice, Pops," Little John said, joining Kaz and Claire across the room.

Pops looked doubtful.

Margaret came back into the living room then. "Claire?" she said. She looked where Claire was looking, but all she saw was an empty wall. "What are you doing?"

"Uh, nothing," Claire said. "I just . . . spaced out for a second."

"Well, come have a snack with us." Margaret grabbed Claire's arm and pulled her into the kitchen.

"I don't think I've ever met a solid who could see ghosts when they weren't glowing," Pops muttered.

"Claire is special," Kaz said.

Pops scowled. "I don't like that you boys are making friends with solids.

Your mother wouldn't like it, either."

"Is Mom here?" Little John asked, looking all around.

"Not in this house," Pops said. "But she's close."

"She is? How do you know?" Kaz asked.

Pops reached into his pocket and pulled out three round ghostly beads.

"Those are from Mom's necklace!" Little John exclaimed.

"I know," Pops said. "I found two of them in other houses on this street. And I found the third one right here in this house. I think I've been following your mother from house to house. I sure wish she'd stay in one place a little longer."

"We've been following her, too," Kaz said. He and Little John reached into their own pockets and pulled out the beads they'd found.

Pops's eyeballs expanded inside his head. "Where did you find those?"

"I found mine in a purple house," Little John said. "There were other ghosts there."

"Other ghosts?" Pops said.

"Yes," Little John replied. "They said Mom had been there, but she wasn't there anymore. They thought maybe she went to the library, so I tried to go there, too.

But it was hard because the wind kept blowing me *past* the library. Eventually I got in by hiding inside a library book. Mom wasn't there. But Kaz and Cosmo were!"

"You know where Cosmo is?" Pops said. Cosmo was the ghost family's dog.

"Yes. He's at the library," Little John said.

Kaz told Pops all about the library, and about meeting Claire, and even about C & K Ghost Detectives.

"We found Cosmo when we investigated one of our first cases," Kaz explained. "And we found Mom's bead when we investigated another case."

"All three of us are on a case right now," Little John put in. He told Pops about Margaret and the other girls and their club. "They meet in a tree house

behind their houses," Little John explained. "But now they think there's a ghost in the tree house. Margaret saw it last night."

"So did I," Pops said.

"You did?" Kaz and Little John said at the same time.

Pops nodded. "I didn't get a real good look at the ghost, but I think it's your mother. I've been glowing on and off to try to get her attention, but she's not glowing back. If only there was a way for ghosts to travel in the Outside without blowing away."

"There is," Little John said with a grin. "Inside Claire's water bottle!"

Pops frowned. "I beg your pardon."

"It's true," Kaz said. "That's how Claire and I go to all our cases."

"No," Pops said. "We don't need help from a solid. And we're certainly not

going to travel inside a water bottle!"

"Why not?" Kaz asked. He'd been traveling inside Claire's water bottle for months. "You know, those girls are probably almost done with their snack. We should check on them. We don't want to miss our ride."

Kaz and Little John swam to the kitchen.

"Wait, boys," Pops said, hurrying after them.

Claire smiled in relief when she saw the ghosts. "There you are," she whispered to Kaz as the other girls stacked their dishes in the sink.

"To the tree house!" Margaret said, raising her fist in the air.

"To the tree house!" Kenya and Olivia repeated as they headed for the back door.

Claire hung back a little to give the ghosts time to swim into her water bottle.

"Boys! I said no. We're not doing this," Pops said as Kaz and Little John shrank down . . . down . . . down and passed through the stars on the outside of Claire's water bottle.

"Come on, Pops!" Little John waved for Pops to join them inside the water bottle.

Pops gaped at Kaz. "Did you just pass through that bottle?"

"Yes," Kaz said nervously.

"When did you learn how to do that?" Pops asked.

Kaz grinned. "I've learned lots of skills since you last saw me," he said. Wait until Pops saw him transform a solid object! But there wasn't time to show Pops that now. Margaret, Olivia, and Kenya were

already outside. And Claire was *almost* outside.

"Hurry, Pops! Come with us before it's too late!" Kaz and Little John yelled.

Pops let out a big breath of air. And at the last possible second, he shrank down . . . down . . . down . . . and swam into the bottle with Kaz and Little John.

CHAPTER 3

TO THE TREE HOUSE

'm your father," Pops said as Claire tromped across Margaret's backyard, her bottle swinging at her side. "When I say we're not going to do something, we're not going to do it."

"Sorry, Pops," Kaz said. "I didn't want to miss our chance to go to the tree house."

"Well, I have to admit this is a very interesting way to travel," Pops said. He turned all around inside the bottle.

Margaret and Henry had a large climbing structure with a swing and two slides in the middle of their backyard. There was also a sandbox and lots of toys.

The girls walked all the way to the trees at the back of the yard. There was a little house built into the branches of the tallest tree. A rope ladder hung from the porch to the ground.

"You're so lucky to have a tree house," Claire said to Margaret.

"I know," Margaret replied.

One by one, the girls climbed the rope ladder. First Margaret, then Kenya, Olivia, and finally, Claire.

"Whoa," Kaz said as Claire climbed higher and higher. The bottle that held the ghosts bumped against her hip as she climbed.

"Uh-oh. Are you skizzy, Kaz?"

Little John asked. "Are you going to spew?" He backed up a little, but he didn't dare move back too far. Otherwise he'd pass through the bottle into the Outside.

"No, I'm not skizzy," Kaz said.

"Then why did you say 'whoa'?" Little John asked.

"Because we're up so high!" Kaz said.

"It's quite a view," Pops said as Claire stepped onto the little porch outside the tree house. They could see Margaret's whole neighborhood from up here.

"We have a lock on the door to keep people out," Margaret told Claire.

Kaz watched from inside the bottle as Margaret spun the dial on the lock. First she turned it to three, then to one, then to five. The lock clicked, and Margaret opened the door.

38

"Cool," Claire said as she followed the other girls inside. They had to crouch down a little because the tree-house door was smaller than a regular door.

As soon as Claire closed the door, the ghosts passed through the side of the bottle and expanded.

"Mom?" Kaz and Little John called as they looked around.

"Elise? Where are you?" Pops called.

The inside of the tree house was all one room. A huge tree branch grew up through the floor and out through the top of one of the walls. Two of the walls had glass windows. There was a rug on the floor and several pillows scattered around.

Kaz and Little John's mom was nowhere in sight.

"Well?" Kenya asked Claire. "Do you see any ghosts?"

"Not yet," Claire said. She unzipped her detective bag and took out her ghost glass and ghost catcher. She put the ghost glass to her eye and moved slowly around the small tree house.

"What is that solid girl doing?" Pops asked.

Kaz explained about Claire's "ghost-hunting equipment." Her ghost glass was really an old magnifying glass. And her ghost catcher was a handheld vacuum that she'd wrapped in foil.

"She can't tell people she can see ghosts," Kaz said. "They'll laugh at her. And they'll think she's weird. So she pretends she needs these things to see and catch ghosts."

Pops snorted. "And other solids believe that?"

"I guess," Kaz said with a shrug.

"Do you see something?" Margaret asked Claire.

"Maybe," Claire said. She glanced over her shoulder and wiggled her eyebrows at Kaz.

What? Did Claire want him to do something? Maybe she was trying to show him something. Unfortunately, Kaz couldn't see through Margaret, Kenya, or Olivia. They'd all crowded around Claire and were trying to see into her ghost glass.

"I don't see anything," Kenya said.

Olivia tossed a braid over her shoulder. "Neither do I," she said.

Kaz floated up and over the girls' heads. Now he could see what Claire was looking at. He drew in a breath.

"What?" Little John asked. "What is it, Kaz?"

Kaz swam over and snatched the small round bead that was floating in the air between Claire's ghost glass and the tree branch. He brought it back to his dad and his little brother.

"This!" he said triumphantly.

"I knew it," Pops said. "Your mother was here."

"But she's not here now," Little John said with disappointment.

"I thought I saw something over here, but I guess I was wrong," Claire said to the other girls. "I don't think there are any ghosts in your tree house right now."

Except for us, Kaz thought.

"Big surprise," Kenya said.

"There may have been a ghost here yesterday," Claire told Margaret.

"There was." Margaret nodded fiercely. "I saw it!"

"Sure," Kenya said, patting Margaret on the back.

"I did!" Margaret said. She looked a little annoyed with Kenya.

Kaz wafted over to one of the windows and scanned Margaret's backyard. Where could his mom have gone?

Claire crawled over to him on her knees. "Sorry, Kaz," she whispered. "I know you must be disappointed."

"What did you say, Claire?" Margaret asked.

"Nothing," Claire said quickly. She smiled innocently at the other girls.

"Oh. I was wondering if you saw something else," Margaret said.

"*I see* something," Kenya said from the other window. The one that looked out over the woods.

"What?" Olivia asked as she, Margaret, and Claire crawled over to Kenya. Kaz, Little John, and Pops floated above them.

Kenya pointed at a boy in the woods. He wore a red cap and a blue jacket. Kaz recognized him from the group of boys they'd seen on the steps next door. He looked younger than Claire and the other girls, or at least shorter. He walked slowly and stared at something in his hand. Probably a phone.

"That's Sam. He's Henry's friend. He lives across the street," Margaret said. She wiggled out of her jacket stuffed it under her knees.

"Yeah, but look over there." Now Kenya pointed at another tree. The other three boys who wouldn't let Henry join their club were now crouched down behind a big tree. They watched Sam with their hands clasped to their mouths, like they were trying not to laugh out loud.

What's so funny? Kaz wondered.

Kenya scowled. "Those boys can be really obnoxious," she said. "I think they're playing some sort of trick on Sam. Like they played a trick on us yesterday by trying to make us think there was a ghost in our tree house."

Margaret watched the boys for a long time. "Maybe," she said finally. "Maybe you're right, Kenya. Maybe I just imagined I saw a ghost out here last night."

Kaz squeezed the bead in his hand. That bead was proof that there *had* been a ghost in here. Maybe not last night. But recently.

They even knew who that ghost was. All they had to do now was find her.

CHAPTER 4

A DANGEROUS IDEA

Get out of that bottle, boys!" Pops said. "Now!"

The ghosts and the girls were all back inside Margaret's kitchen. Claire had just put her ghost glass and ghost catcher back inside her bag and was getting ready to go home.

"No," Little John said stubbornly.

Kaz didn't want to disobey Pops again. But Pops didn't understand. "We want to go back to the library with Claire," Kaz

said in a small voice. "The library is our new haunt."

"Yeah," Little John said. "Cosmo is there, and Beckett."

"Who's Beckett?" Pops asked.

"He's the other ghost who lives at the library," Kaz said.

"Beckett will wonder where we are," Little John said.

"Sorry, boys," Pops said. "We're not going anywhere until we find your mother." He reached into Claire's water bottle and pulled Kaz and Little John out.

"But Claire can help us find Mom," Little John said.

"We don't need help from a solid girl," Pops said.

"What about Cosmo?" Kaz asked. "Are we just going to leave him in the library all alone?"

"He's not alone," Pops said. "You just said he's with your friend Beckett."

"Is something wrong, Claire?" Olivia asked as Claire watched the ghosts.

Claire blinked. "No. I'm fine," she said to the girls. She threw the strap of her bag over her shoulder and gave Kaz a rueful look. "I better go. It's almost time for dinner."

Little John groaned. Kaz bit his lip. They really weren't going with Claire?

"We're not mad that you didn't find any ghosts, if that's what you're thinking," Kenya said as she put a hand on Claire's shoulder. "I don't think there are any ghosts for you to find."

"I'll let you know if any ghosts come back," Margaret promised.

Pops sighed when he saw how unhappy Kaz and Little John were.

"Maybe when we find your mother, we can make our way to the library," he said.

Little John perked up. "We just have to glow and wail a bit when we want to go to the library," he said. "Then Margaret will call Claire, and Claire will come and get us!"

"Hey, that's good thinking, Little John," Kaz said, feeling a little better about the situation.

"Bye," Claire said to the girls *and* the ghosts. She raised her hand, and Kaz touched his hand to hers. It passed right on through.

"See you soon," he said.

* * * * * * * * * * * * * * *

That night while Margaret and Henry and their parents slept in their bedrooms upstairs, Kaz wailed softly in the living room below them. "Woo . . . ooo . . . ooo . . . ooo!"

"That's very good, son!" Pops said, clapping his hands together.

All of a sudden, a voice rang out above them: "MOOOOOOOMMMMM!"

"Oh no," Kaz moaned as the upstairs hallway light came on and shined down the stairs.

The ghosts listened as Margaret and

Henry's mom called out, "What's the matter, Henry? Are you sick?"

"No," Henry called back. "I heard a ghost."

"Way to go, Kaz," Little John said as he slugged Kaz in the arm.

"I didn't mean for anyone other than you guys to hear me," Kaz said.

"Then why did you wail?" Little John asked. "That's the whole point of wailing. So solids can hear us."

"I wanted to show Pops that I could do it," Kaz said. Clearly, that was a bad idea.

Margaret and Henry's mom said, "Oh, honey. You had a bad dream. There's no such thing as ghosts."

The ghosts looked at one another. "Why do solids always say there's no such thing as ghosts?" Pops muttered.

"Look what else I can do," Kaz said. He dived down to the floor and picked up a solid toy car.

"Wow," Pops said as Kaz held the solid car in his ghostly hands.

"Wait. I'm not done," Kaz said. He held the car between his third finger and his thumb, then flicked his wrist. The solid car became a ghostly car.

"WOW!" Pops said again. He swam over and poked the ghostly car with his finger. "You have the transformation skill."

"You know about transformation?" Kaz asked.

"Of course," Pops said. "But I didn't know anyone in our family had the skill."

"MOOOOOOOMMMMM!" Henry yelled again above them.

"Now what?" his mom called back.

The ghosts raised their eyes toward the ceiling. Henry didn't somehow *know* that Kaz had transformed his car, did he? Was that why he had yelled for his mom? Just in case, Kaz quickly transformed the ghostly car back to a solid car.

"THERE'S A GHOST OUTSIDE," Henry yelled, "IN THE TREE HOUSE!"

"A ghost in the tree house!" Pops repeated. He, Little John, and Kaz paddled hard through the dining room and into the kitchen. They went to the

window and saw a ghostly glow coming from inside the tree house.

"Is that Mom?" Little John asked, wide-eyed. "Is she back?"

"Looks like it," Pops said.

The ghostly glow went out.

"Where'd she go? Did she leave?" Kaz asked.

The ghosts stared hard at the tree house, waiting for the glow to return. Pops even glowed on and off a couple of times in the window to get the other ghost's attention.

The glow didn't return.

"We need to find a way to get out to the tree house," Kaz said as he looked around the kitchen for something they could use to travel across the backyard.

"Margaret said she'd let Claire know if the ghost came back," Little John said.

"Maybe she's calling Claire right now. Maybe Claire will come and take us there."

"Not now," Kaz said. "It's the middle of the night."

"Then maybe Margaret and Henry's mom and dad will go out to the tree house," Little John said. "Maybe we can catch a ride with them?"

But no one came downstairs.

"I think I have an idea," Pops said as he gazed out across the moonlit yard.

"What?" Little John asked. "What's your idea, Pops?"

Pops turned to the boys. "I'm trying to decide whether or not we should risk it," he said. "It could be dangerous. *Very* dangerous."

CHAPTER 5

EXP-A-A-A-ND

T ell us the idea!" Little John begged Pops. "We're not afraid of danger. Are we, Kaz?"

Well . . . , Kaz thought. But out loud he said, "No. We're not afraid of danger." He could be brave if it meant finding his mom. The sooner they found Mom, the sooner they could go back to the library.

"How far can you boys expand?" Pops asked.

"Pretty far," Little John said proudly. He exp-a-a-a-a-nded from the floor almost to the ceiling to prove it.

"Fabulous. How about you, Kaz?" Pops asked.

Kaz was taller than Little John. He exp-a-a-a-a-nded from the floor and *past* the ceiling. His head popped through the ceiling and into Margaret's bedroom upstairs.

Margaret was sound asleep in her bed.

"Very good," Pops said as Kaz and Little John shrank to their normal sizes.

He peered out into the backyard. "This could work."

"What could work? What do you want us to do?" Kaz asked.

"Yeah, what's your idea, Pops?" Little John asked.

"If we all expand as far as we can, and then hold hands really, really tight, we *might* be able to stretch from inside this house all the way to the tree house," Pops said.

"You mean expand across the whole backyard?" Kaz asked. That did sound dangerous.

"Let's try!" Little John said eagerly.

"Okay. I'll stay here in the house and make sure we don't all blow into the Outside," Pops said. "Little John, you'll go first. I want you to hold tight to Kaz's hand. Then you're going to pass through

this window and expand into the backyard as far as you can. Kaz, you'll grab my hand with your other hand, and then you'll pass through and expand as far as you can. Finally, I'll expand my arm, Little John, and we'll see if you can reach the tree house. If your mother is there, she can grab onto your hand, and we'll pull her back here."

"That sounds like a good plan," Little John said.

But if anyone let go, or if Pops wasn't strong enough to keep his body inside the house while holding onto Kaz's hand outside the house, they would all blow away!

Kaz remembered how their big brother, Finn, used to stick his arm or leg through the walls of the old schoolhouse because he liked to scare his little brothers. But one day Finn wasn't strong enough to keep the rest

of his body inside the old schoolhouse. The wind pulled him into the Outside, and he blew away.

Grandmom and Grandpop had tried to rescue him, but they ended up in the Outside, too. Kaz and Claire had found his grandparents at a nursing home near the library a few weeks ago.

But no one, including Grandmom and Grandpop, knew what had happened to Finn.

"We can do it. Right, Kaz?" Little John said as he reached for Kaz's hand.

Kaz gulped. They had to try. "Right," he said.

"Okay, let's do this," Pops said. He grabbed Kaz's other hand.

Kaz held tight to both hands as Little John passed slowly through the glass window and exp-a-a-a-a-nded out . . .

out . . . out . . . across Margaret and Henry's backyard.

"Hey, it's raining out here!" Little John called from the Outside. "I've never felt raindrops pass through me before." He giggled.

Great, Kaz thought. He didn't know what Little John was giggling about. He remembered the first time he was inside Claire's water bottle and she turned on the water above him. He didn't like it when the water passed through his body. He didn't like it at all.

"Your turn, Kaz," Pops said. "Are you

ready? You've learned to do so many things since we've been apart. Wait until your mother sees everything you can do now."

Kaz gulped again. He could do this. For his mom.

He took a deep breath, then followed Little John through the window and out . . . out . . . out . . . across the yard. Rain pounded through his head. His arms. His back. It felt like little bits of him were being dropped all over the yard. But Kaz managed to hold himself together and push his brother farther into the yard.

Then Pops exp-a-a-a-a-nded his arm and pushed Kaz and Little John even farther. But Little John still wasn't past the backyard climbing structure.

"Can you guys expand any more?" Little John asked as lightning flashed and thunder rumbled above them.

"I'll try," Pops said.

Kaz could feel Pops pushing . . . pushing . . . pushing. He str-e-e-e-e-tched both arms as far as he could. But it still wasn't enough.

"I can't expand any more," Kaz said, exhausted from the effort.

"Neither can I," Little John said.

Kaz felt Little John's grip loosen. "No! Don't let go!" he yelled as he squeezed his brother's hand as tight as he could.

"I'm not!" Little John said. Holding firmly to Kaz's hand, he tried kicking his

legs. But that didn't get him any closer to the tree house either.

"MOOOOOOOMMMMM!" Little John yelled like Henry had yelled a little while ago. "ARE YOU IN THE TREE HOUSE?"

If she was, she didn't answer.

* * * * * * * * * * * * * * *

"My shoulders hurt," Little John said the next morning.

"Mine too," Kaz said.

"I'm a little stiff myself," Pops said as he rubbed his shoulders. "We're not used to expanding so far."

"Or for so long," Little John added.

The ghosts hovered above Margaret, Henry, and their parents, who were eating breakfast. The parents seemed very tired this morning.

All of a sudden, Margaret bolted from her chair. "I left my jacket in the tree house yesterday," she said.

Little John gasped. "She's going to the tree house," he said.

"We have to go with her," Kaz said.

But how could they do that? Margaret didn't have a water bottle or anything the ghosts could travel in. And she was out the door before the ghosts knew what to do.

They watched helplessly from the window as she ran across her backyard.

She scrambled up the rope ladder, fumbled with the lock, and went inside the tree house.

She wasn't in there for long. Three seconds at most. She locked the tree house back up, scrambled down the ladder, and then raced across the yard with her blue jacket dangling from her arm.

She banged the back door open. "Guess what?" she said breathlessly. "The ghost is back!"

CHAPTER 6

●●●● ●●,
— — — ——!

told you!" Henry said. "I told you I saw a ghost in the tree house last night. And I told you I heard a ghost in our house!"

"There's no such thing as ghosts," Henry's dad said as he turned a page in his newspaper.

"No one ever believes me," Henry grumbled.

"I believe you," Margaret said. "I've seen a ghost in the tree house, too.

I didn't see it last night, but I believe you saw it. It tracked in mud and messed up the pillows. That's how I know it was there last night."

Henry shifted in his seat a little.

"Wait. Ghosts don't track in mud," Kaz said. "We don't walk on the ground, so our feet don't ever get muddy."

But Kaz and Little John and Pops had all seen the ghost glowing in the tree house during the night, too.

"Maybe you girls tracked in the mud yourselves when you were in there yesterday afternoon," Margaret's mom suggested.

"We didn't," Margaret said. "I know we didn't because the ground was dry yesterday afternoon. It didn't rain until last night."

"Maybe someone went in after it

started raining?" Dad suggested.

"How would they have gotten in? The door is locked!" Margaret said.

"Ghosts can walk through walls," Henry said.

"Maybe you didn't lock the door. Or maybe someone figured out the combination," Mom said.

"No one knows the combination except people in this family and Kenya and Olivia," Margaret said.

Henry bit his lip.

"Okay, kids. Time to get ready for school," Dad said.

They all got up from the table and went to gather their things.

When no one else was looking, Kaz saw Henry kick a pair of shoes under the bench by the back door. Then Henry sat down and put on a different pair of shoes.

Kaz peered under the bench. He saw that the shoes Henry had kicked under there had mud on them.

But that didn't make any sense. Henry was in his bedroom when they all saw the ghost in the tree house last night.

* * * * * * * * * * * * *

Kaz, Little John, and Pops spent the rest of the morning near the kitchen window, watching the tree house.

But if the ghost was still out there, she wasn't showing herself.

"Margaret said she'd let Claire know if the ghost came back," Kaz said. "Maybe Claire will come home with Margaret after school, and she'll take us back to the tree house."

"Oh, I hope so," Little John said.

Pops sniffed. "We can solve this problem on our own," he said.

But as morning turned to afternoon, neither Pops nor Kaz nor Little John had figured out a way to get to the tree house. They didn't even know whether the ghost was still out there. They hadn't seen any more glowing.

A few hours later, Margaret and Henry came home with their mom. First they had a snack in the kitchen. Then Margaret and Henry turned on the computer and started a game that had something to do with zapping bugs.

"This is how solid children spend their time?" Pops said as he stared at the screen.

"It looks fun!" Little John said.

"It looks . . . dull," Pops said. Yet he couldn't seem to tear himself away.

All of a sudden, the doorbell rang. Was it Claire?

"I'll get it," Margaret said. She raced to the door. Kaz floated behind her.

It wasn't Claire. It was Kenya and Olivia.

Kaz groaned. Maybe Claire was still coming. He swam to the window and looked up and down the street. He didn't see Claire, but he saw those same older boys sitting on the grass next door. They had a gray metal case in front of them and a bucket of small objects. But Kaz couldn't tell what any of that stuff was.

"So, what are we going to do about this ghost?" Olivia asked.

"Maybe we should call that Claire girl again," Margaret said.

Yes! Kaz thought, turning toward the girls. *Call Claire! Call her right now.*

"It's not a ghost," Kenya said.

"Then what is it?" Margaret asked. "I'm not the only one who's seen it. My brother saw it last night. And this morning there was mud on the rug in our tree house. But the door was still locked. How did someone get in through a locked door? It has to be a ghost."

Kenya shrugged. "Or someone who knows the combination to the lock."

"Who knows the combination besides us?" Margaret asked.

Kenya strolled over to the window. Kaz darted out of her way.

74

"Maybe one of them," Kenya said, pointing at the boys next door. Margaret and Olivia went to see who she was taking about.

"I didn't tell them the combination," Margaret said.

"Neither did I," Olivia said. She pressed closer to the window. "What are those boys doing, anyway?"

"They're making treasure boxes," Henry said without looking up from

his game. "That's what they do in their club. They make treasure boxes and hide them in the woods. Then they use a special app on their phones to find treasure boxes that other people hid."

"Let's go talk to them," Kenya said. "We'll see if any of them know the combination to our lock."

Margaret snorted. "How do you know they'll tell us the truth?"

"I'm pretty good at knowing when people are telling the truth and when they're not," Kenya said. "Let's go!"

"Wait!" Henry pressed a button on the keyboard, and the game froze. He hopped down from his chair. "Can I go, too?" he asked.

Pops swam closer to the computer screen. "What happened?" he asked. "Why did the game stop?"

"Henry paused it," Kaz explained.

"But there are more bugs to zap," Pops said.

Little John giggled. "I thought you said it was a dull game."

"It . . . is," Pops said. "I just think that solid boy should finish what he starts."

"They aren't going to let you join their club, Henry," Margaret said as she tied her shoe.

"They might," Henry said, "if I help Sam find the treasure."

Margaret sighed. "Fine. You can come. But if they aren't nice to you, don't say I didn't warn you. Mom?" she called. "We're going next door. Henry's coming, too."

"Okay," their mom called back.

"Can we go with them?" Little John asked.

"I'd like to," Kaz replied. But he didn't see how they could. Again, none of the girls was carrying anything the ghosts could travel in.

Margaret opened the front door, and the ghosts plunged backward so they wouldn't be pulled into the Outside. As soon as the door closed, they swam to the window.

There was a whole crowd of kids next door now: Margaret, Kenya, Olivia, Henry, his friend Sam, and the three older boys.

Kaz wished he could hear what all those kids were saying.

Henry and Sam didn't stay with the older kids for long. All of a sudden, they ran across the street and disappeared inside Sam's house.

Pops gasped. "Look at that." He

pointed at the house. "Do you see who's in the window?"

Kaz didn't see anyone in the window at first. But he was looking at the wrong window.

"The upstairs window," Pops said. A big smile spread across his face.

"Ohhhhh," Little John said.

"It's Mom!" Kaz exclaimed. He waved at her, and she waved back.

Mom glowed on and off several times. On and off. On and off. On and off.

Pops laughed. Then he started glowing on and off. On and off. On and off. So did Little John. Kaz felt left out because he couldn't glow.

But as Kaz watched his parents and his brother, he realized his parents were glowing differently than Little John was. Some of their glows were long. Some of them were short. It was almost like they were talking to each other.

"Are you and Mom talking to each other in a secret code?" Kaz asked.

"We are," Pops grinned. "It's Morse code. We used to do this when we were young ghosts, and your mother's haunt was across the street from mine."

Little John stopped glowing. "What's Morse code?"

"It's a code that uses short and long signals to make the letters," Pops explained.

International MORSE CODE

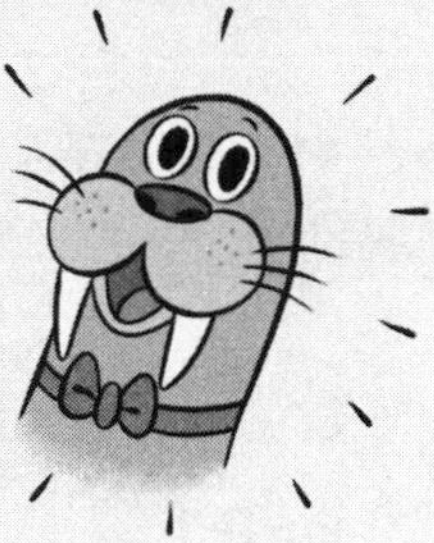

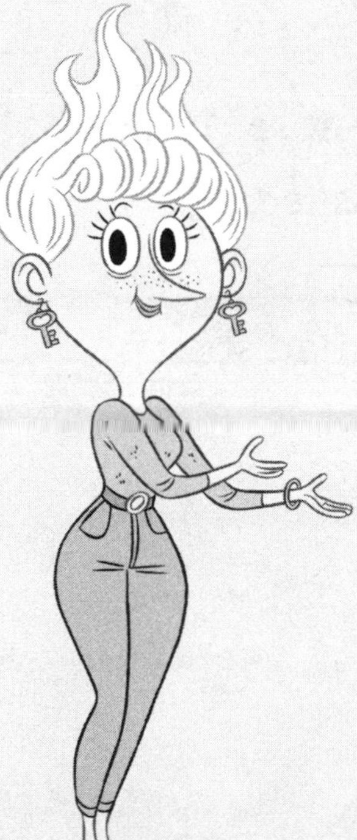

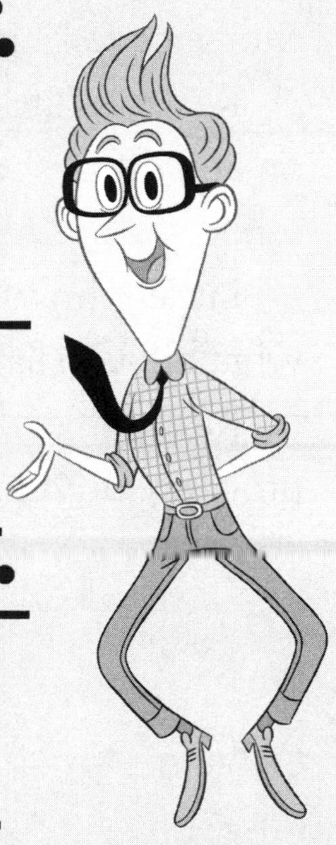

A	•—
B	—•••
C	—•—•
D	—••
E	•
F	••—•
G	——•
H	••••
I	••
J	•———
K	—•—
L	•—••
M	——
N	—•
O	———
P	•——•
Q	——•—
R	•—•
S	•••
T	—
U	••—
V	•••—
W	•——
X	—••—
Y	—•——
Z	——••

"You've heard of SOS, right?" He glowed short-short-short, then long-long-long, then short-short-short. "SOS means help!"

"Yes. But I didn't know that was Morse code," Little John said.

Kaz and Little John's parents glowed on and off in short and long bursts for a while.

Little John wrinkled his nose. "Now what are you saying?" he asked.

Kaz nudged his brother. "It's probably private mom and dad stuff."

CHAPTER 7

TRADING STORIES

"N o fair talking in a code we don't know," Little John whined. "Plus, *I* want to talk to Mom, too!"

"Your mom thinks we should stop talking for a while," Pops said. "There are a lot of solid children out and about. She's afraid they'll notice us." He hovered in the window and glowed three long glows, then one long, one short, and one more long glow.

"Long-long-long," Little John said,

"and long-short-long. What does that spell?"

"It spells OK," Pops said. "Long-long-long is *O*. And long-short-long is *K*. I'll teach you the whole alphabet, Little John, but not right now. We have to figure out a way to rescue your mom."

"If Claire were here, she could help us," Kaz said.

"We don't need help from solids. We are perfectly capable of rescuing your mother ourselves!" Pops said.

How? Kaz wondered.

"We need something to travel in," Pops said. "Something hollow with a lid. Like a bottle or a box."

There were several things in the room that could work. A covered coffee cup. A plastic box that had farm animals inside. A toy drum. If the drum was hollow on the inside . . .

Kaz shrank down . . . down . . . down . . . and passed through the side of the drum. It was hollow.

"Good idea, Kaz," Pops called from outside the drum. "We can travel in there."

Kaz passed through the outside of the toy drum and returned to the living room. "We could . . . *if* we had someone to carry the drum across the street," he said. *Someone like Claire.*

Pops scratched his head. "What if only one of us goes inside the drum, and the others stay here and roll it across the street?"

"How do we get it out the door?" Kaz asked.

"You could transform it," Little John said. "Then it could roll through the wall!"

Kaz peered out the window. "Yeah, but then it would just blow away in the wind," he said, "With one of us inside."

"Oh," Little John said, hanging his head. "That would be bad."

Pops sighed. "Maybe we *do* need help from a solid."

"When Margaret comes back, let's glow and wail and tell her to call Claire," Little John said.

Pops nodded. "Okay," he said.

But the ghosts didn't have to wait for Margaret to come back. And they didn't have to ask her to call Claire.

Henry came back before Margaret did. He carried a red case in his arms.

"What's that you've got there, Henry?" his mom asked when he came in.

"Some cars," Henry said. "Sam's letting me borrow them." He dropped to his knees and opened the case upside down. "See?"

It wasn't just cars that came tumbling out of the case. Kaz and Little John's mom wafted out, too.

"Mom!" the ghosts shouted as she expanded to her normal size. They hugged and kissed and danced around.

"I'm so happy to see you all!" Mom said.

"Us too!" said Pops. "I knew you were nearby. I found beads from your necklace." He reached into his pocket and pulled out three ghostly blue beads.

"We found some beads, too. Didn't we, Kaz?" Little John said.

Kaz nodded.

"I found one at the purple house where Kiley and those other ghosts lived," Little John said.

Mom's face glowed in surprise. "You met those ghosts?"

"Yes," Little John replied. "They told me you'd been there. Why did you leave?"

"I was looking for all of you," Mom said.

Pops frowned. "You should've stayed in one place. Then we would've found

you instead of all those beads from your necklace."

"I didn't want to. I wanted to do something," Mom said. "I was determined to find someone in the family before I ran out of beads." She reached into her pocket

 and pulled out what was left of her necklace. There were only five beads left.

"Well, you found us!" Kaz said.

"How did you know to go inside that case?" Little John asked. "How did you know Henry would bring the case over here?"

"Because I've been watching the solid children," Mom replied. "I knew that the boy named Henry lived in this house. And I'd just seen you all in the window. So when Sam asked Henry if he wanted to borrow some cars, I saw my chance!"

They packed up the case, and I swam inside. It was the only way I knew to travel safely in the Outside."

"It seems our boys have been doing quite a bit of traveling in the Outside," Pops said in a grumbly voice.

"Oh?" Mom turned to Kaz and Little John with surprise.

Pops folded his arms. "They've made friends with a solid girl," he said.

"WHAT?" Mom shrieked. "No! You boys wouldn't be that foolish, would you?"

"It's not foolish," Little John said. "It's nice. Claire's nice!"

"She can see us when we're not glowing and she can hear us when we're not wailing," Kaz explained. "And she takes us everywhere inside her water bottle."

"Hmm," Mom said. "That sounds dangerous."

"It's not," Kaz said. Then he told his mom about C & K Ghost Detectives and all the cases he and Claire had solved. "None of our cases have led to any real ghosts. But we still found Cosmo, and Grandmom and Grandpop, and now you guys!"

"You know where Grandmom and Grandpop are?" Mom asked.

"Yes," Little John said. "They're at an old folks' home. Claire takes us to visit them. There are lots of solids there who can see ghosts. Grandmom and Grandpop have made friends with solids, too."

"Maybe we should meet this solid girl," Mom said.

"I've met her," Pops said. "I've even traveled inside her water bottle."

Mom's eyebrows shot up. "You have?"

"Yes," Pops admitted. "The boys wanted to go to the tree house and rescue you. So I went with them. That was yesterday."

"Yesterday?" Mom said. She wafted into the kitchen where she could see the tree house. Kaz, Little John, and Pops followed close behind.

"I did spend a little time in that tree house," Mom said. "But not yesterday. That was several days ago."

"You weren't there yesterday afternoon. But you were there last night, weren't you?" Pops asked.

"We saw you," Little John said.

Mom shook her head. "You didn't see me," she said. "I haven't been there in at least three days."

"Then who did we see?" Kaz asked.

* * * * * * * * * * * * * * *

The ghost family talked long into the night. They hardly noticed Margaret's family eating dinner or cleaning up the kitchen around them.

Kaz showed his mom all the new ghost skills he'd learned since they'd been apart.

"That's wonderful, Kaz," Mom said. "I'm so proud of you."

He and Little John told their parents about the library. And the secret room.

After the solid family turned out the lights and went up to bed, Mom and Pops shared stories about where they'd been since the old schoolhouse was torn down. They'd both been drifting from place to place, trying to find their family. Mom had spent time in a clothing store, a school (Claire's school!), and several houses. She'd heard there were ghosts in the library, but she had never managed to find the library.

Pops had spent time in an old barn, a farmhouse, a motel, and now this house. He hadn't run into any other ghosts like Kaz, Little John, and Mom had. He was the only one who hadn't.

"There must not be a lot of ghosts in this part of town," Mom said.

"We know there's at least one," Little John said as he glanced out the kitchen window. "And guess what? It's in the tree house right now!"

CHAPTER 8

DON'T SCARE MARGARET

Who is it? Who is that ghost?" Mom asked as they gathered around the window.

A ghostly light bounced around the tree house. Just like the other night.

"Maybe it's Finn," Little John said. Finn was the only ghost in their family they hadn't found yet.

Pops tried glowing on and off in short and long bursts: short-short-short-short. Short. Short-long-short-short.

Short-long-short-short. Long-long-long.

"What are you saying?" Little John asked.

"He's saying hello," Mom said.

"Does Finn know Morse code?" Kaz asked.

"I don't know," Mom replied. She turned to Pops. "We should teach the boys Morse code."

"We should," Pops agreed. "Then they could talk to us if we get separated again."

The ghost in the tree house drifted back and forth in front of the window. He didn't stop at the window long enough for Kaz and his family to get a good look at him. And he didn't respond to the Morse code message.

"We need to find a way to get back to the tree house," Pops said. "That's the

only way we're going to find out who's in there."

"We could wake Margaret up and tell her to call Claire," Little John suggested. "Claire would take us to the tree house."

"We can't call Claire in the middle of the night," Kaz said, throwing his hands into the air.

"Why not ask the solid girl to take us to the tree house herself?" Mom suggested.

"She doesn't see or hear ghosts like Claire does," Kaz said. "If we start glowing and wailing in the middle of the night, we might scare her."

"Do you have to say no to every single idea we think of?" Little John asked.

"I'm not really saying no," Kaz said. "I'm saying we have to be careful how

we ask her. We don't want to scare her. It's nighttime. Solid kids are even more scared of things at night."

"Kaz, maybe you or Little John should talk to her," Mom said. "You're kids like she is. She's less likely to be scared of another kid."

"I'll do it," Little John cried out as he shot toward the ceiling.

"No," Kaz said, grabbing his brother by the foot and pulling him back. "*I'll* do it. You're not exactly subtle, Little John."

Little John clucked his tongue. "I can be subtle," he said.

Mom put her arm around Little John. "Let's let Kaz do this, okay?"

"Fine," Little John said. "Can we at least go with him?"

"Only if you're quiet. And you don't glow," Kaz said.

Kaz swam up to the ceiling and passed through into Margaret's bedroom. Little John, Mom, and Pops passed through right behind him.

Margaret was sound asleep, snoring in her bed.

Kaz drifted over. "Ghost . . . ," he wailed softly into her ear. "Ghost . . . in . . . the . . . tree . . . house . . ."

Margaret slept on.

Little John snorted. "There's such a thing as being *too* subtle, you know."

"Shh!" Mom said, squeezing Little John's shoulders.

"Why? She can't hear us," Little John said.

"Ghost . . . ," Kaz wailed again. "Ghost . . . in . . . the . . . tree . . . house . . ."

This time Margaret rolled over.

"There's . . . a . . . ghost . . . in . . . the . . . tree . . . house . . . ," Kaz wailed. "Go . . . there . . .

"Go . . . to . . . your . . . tree . . . house . . . Go . . . to . . . your . . . tree . . . house . . . and . . . bring . . . a . . . water . . . bottle . . . with . . . you . . . Put . . . some . . . water . . . in . . . the . . . bottle . . . You . . . can . . . pour . . . the . . . water . . . on . . . the . . . ghost . . ."

"Kaz!" Mom, Pops, and Little John said at the same time.

"What are you saying?" Mom cried out in shock.

"I'm trying to give her a reason to

bring a water bottle with her," Kaz said. "So we can travel inside it."

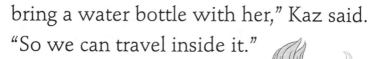

Margaret tossed her blankets aside and walked sleepily over to her window. Kaz wondered if she was even awake as he and the rest of his family drifted around her.

The tree house was dark.

* * * * * * * * * * * * * * * *

Margaret went back to bed. The tree house remained dark the rest of the night.

When Margaret woke up the next

morning, Kaz wailed to her again. A new message: "Get . . . Claire . . . Get . . . Claire . . ."

Margaret's eyes grew wide. "Who said that? Is there a ghost in my room?"

"Yes . . . ," Kaz wailed. "I . . . won't . . . hurt . . . you . . . Just . . . bring . . . Claire . . ."

Margaret grabbed her backpack and scurried away. Kaz hoped Margaret got the message.

The ghosts had Margaret and Henry's house to themselves for most of the day. Mom watched the tree house for signs of a ghost. Kaz and Little John played with Margaret's and Henry's toys. And Pops figured out how to turn on the computer and get into Henry's bug-zapping game.

When Margaret came home, Claire was not with her.

"Darn," Kaz said.

After dinner, the doorbell rang. Kenya and Olivia came in with small suitcases and sleeping bags.

Still no Claire.

Then the doorbell rang again. This time it was Claire. Like Kenya and Olivia, she carried a small suitcase in one hand and a sleeping bag under the other arm. She also had her detective bag on her back and her water bottle draped over her shoulder.

"Finally, you're back!" Kaz said.

Claire grinned at Kaz. Her eyes widened at the sight of Kaz's mother behind him.

"Claire," Kaz said. "This is my mom. Mom, this is Claire!"

"Nice to meet you," Kaz's mom said politely. She kept a bit of distance between herself and the solid girls.

Claire couldn't really talk to the ghosts in front of Margaret, Kenya, and

Olivia. "Thanks for inviting me to your sleepover!" she said to Margaret as she adjusted the sleeping bag under her arm.

"I'm glad you could come," Margaret said.

The girls trooped into the kitchen with all their things. Kaz, Little John, and their parents wafted after them.

"Are you girls sure you want to sleep in the tree house?" Margaret's mother asked.

"Yes," they chorused.

"We're going to catch a ghost tonight," Margaret added.

"Or . . . we're going to catch some boys pretending to be ghosts," Kenya put in.

"Well, I'll leave the back door open in case you want to come back in during the night," Margaret's mom said. "Wait! Don't forget flashlights."

"All set," Claire said, patting her bag.

Margaret opened a cabinet under the sink and pulled out two more flashlights. She stuck one in her pocket and handed the other to Olivia.

"Let's go!" Kaz said. He and Little John shrank down . . . down . . . down . . . and passed through the side of Claire's water bottle.

Kaz's mom looked a little unsure.

"It's okay, Elise," Pops said. "I've done this before." He reached for Mom's hand, and the two ghosts shrank down . . . down . . . down . . . and passed through the bottle.

It was a little crowded with four ghosts, so they all shrank a little more.

"Let's go catch a ghost!" Margaret said as she opened the back door.

CHAPTER 9

A GOOD PLACE TO HIDE

It was starting to get dark outside. Margaret climbed the rope ladder first, and the other girls passed their suitcases, sleeping bags, and flashlights up to her. She piled everything on the porch and unlocked the door.

The other girls climbed the ladder, grabbed their things, and crawled inside the tree house. Claire closed the door behind them and turned on her flashlight. Kaz, Little John, Mom, and Pops passed through the water bottle and expanded partway back to their normal sizes. It was too crowded to expand all the way.

They looked around, but didn't see any other ghosts in the tree house.

"Maybe the ghost is hiding," Little John said.

"Where?" Kaz asked.

"I don't know." Little John shrugged. "But he always comes back. So maybe he never really leaves."

It was a possibility, Kaz thought.

Where could a ghost hide in here?

"What makes you so sure there's a ghost in this tree house, Margaret?" Kenya asked as she plopped down on a red pillow. Olivia plopped down on a green pillow beside her. Margaret and Claire unrolled their sleeping bags.

"I don't know if I dreamed this or it really happened," Margaret said. "But last night while I was asleep, I heard this voice. It said there was a ghost in the tree house."

"That was me," Kaz told Claire.

"It wanted me to go out to the tree house and bring a water bottle that was half full of water and then pour the water on the ghost," Margaret added.

Kenya and Olivia giggled.

Claire shot Kaz a look.

"I can explain—" he started to say.

"That had to be a dream," Olivia said to Margaret.

"I thought so, too," Margaret said. "I got up and went to the window, but I didn't see anything in the tree house. I've definitely seen a ghost out here other nights, though. So has Henry. Then this morning, I heard a ghost in my room. It wasn't in the tree house anymore. It was in *my room*. It told me to get Claire."

"How does it know Claire's name?" Olivia asked.

"Wait." Kenya held up her hand. "You think the ghost is in your house now?" she asked Margaret. "Then what are we doing out here?"

Margaret threw her hands into the air. "I don't know if it's in my house. I don't know if it's out here. I don't know where it is!"

"But you saw a ghost inside your house this morning? For real?" Olivia asked.

"Well . . . I didn't see it. I heard it," Margaret said.

"How do you know it was a ghost?" Kenya asked.

"Because it told me it was!" Margaret said.

Kenya looked doubtful.

Claire stretched her legs out in front of her. "We'll see if any ghosts visit us tonight," she said. "If not, it'll still be fun to sleep in a tree house."

Kaz and his family floated around the tree house. Mom stopped in front of one window and peered outside. Pops hovered in front of the other window. Kaz and Little John drifted back and forth above the girls.

"I wonder if that tree branch is hollow on the inside," Little John said out of the blue.

The other ghosts and Claire all turned toward the branch.

"Hmm," Kaz said. "If it is, that would be a good place for a ghost to hide."

Kaz stuck his arm inside the branch. "It feels hollow," he said. He shrank down . . . down . . . down . . . then passed through the bark of the branch.

"Our Kaz has gotten so brave," Mom said from the tree house.

Having his parents and Claire so close made Kaz *feel* brave. He blinked his eyes a couple of times to adjust to the darkness, then looked around. He was inside a narrow, hollow tunnel inside the tree branch. Bits of dirt and dust clung to the inside of the branch.

Kaz shrank down . . . down . . . down . . . down a little more, and swam headfirst through the tunnel.

"Hello?" he called. "Is there anyone in here?"

He didn't see any ghosts.

He swam a little farther, until he came to a metal box that seemed to be blocking most of the rest of the tunnel. Kaz didn't dare get too close to it. He could feel air from the Outside coming up around the sides of the box. That meant there was probably an opening to the Outside on the other side of the box.

Kaz turned a somersault and started to swim back the way he had come.

He stopped swimming when he heard a loud SCREAM above him.

Mom, Pops, and Little John suddenly appeared inside the tunnel with him.

"What's going on?" Kaz asked as he swam in place.

"The ghost is back," Little John said. "Only it's not a ghost. It's a kid with a flashlight!"

"Who?" Kaz asked.

Little John shrugged. "All we saw was the flashlight. Whoever it was just opened the door and came in. Then those girls started screaming and shuffling around."

"The intruder backed off right away," Pops said. "Who wouldn't with all the noise those girls were making? At least one of the girls ran after him. The others started to open the windows. That's when we passed through the branch. We didn't want to blow into the Outside."

Mom wrung her hands together. "Those solid girls will probably go back inside their house after they catch the intruder," she moaned. "And then we'll be stuck inside this tree forever."

"No, we won't," Kaz said. "Claire won't leave us here. She'll come back and rescue us."

"Are you sure about that?" Mom asked.

"Positive," Kaz said.

CHAPTER 10

CAUGHT!

K az?" Claire called from outside the tree branch. "The door and windows are closed. You guys can come out now. But hurry!"

"See?" Kaz said to his family. "I told you Claire would come back." He swam through the branch and back into the tree house. Little John, Mom, and Pops swam behind him.

"I knew she'd rescue us," Little John said as he started to expand.

"No, don't expand," Claire said. She held out her water bottle. "Quick! Get in here." She strained to see out the window as she spoke to the ghosts. "I think Margaret and Kenya caught the person who tried to break in. I want to see who it is."

"We do, too!" Kaz said as he passed through the side of the bottle. Little John, Mom, and Pops were right behind him.

Claire flung the strap around her neck, then hurried out the door and down the rope ladder. When she was close to the ground, she jumped the rest of the way.

It was dark outside, but a light on Margaret's house lit up much of the backyard.

"I'll bet life is always an adventure with this girl," Mom said as Claire raced across the yard.

"Um . . . sort of," Kaz said. But adventure was a good thing, wasn't it?

Claire caught up to the other girls over by the climbing structure. Olivia and Kenya had hold of someone: Henry's friend, Sam.

Margaret stood in front of him with her arms crossed. "Why were you trying to break into our tree house?" she asked.

"I told you. I'm trying to find the

treasure," Sam said, lunging forward. But Olivia and Kenya held tight to his arms. "I have to find the treasure before I can join the treasure hunters' club."

"There's no treasure in our tree house," Margaret said.

"My phone says there is," Sam insisted. "I'll show you if you let go of me."

Olivia and Kenya exchanged a look.

"Okay. Show us," Olivia said as they let go. But they were both ready to grab him again if he ran away.

Sam reached into his jacket pocket and pulled out his phone.

"That's a pretty nice phone for a kid your age," Kenya said.

"It's my dad's old phone," Sam said with a shrug. "He got a new one." He turned on the phone, and the screen gave off a bluish glow.

Like a glowing ghost, Kaz thought.

Sam slid his finger around the screen, then held the phone for the girls to see. Unfortunately, Kaz and his family couldn't see the screen from inside Claire's water bottle.

"The green dot shows where we are, and the red dot shows where the treasure is," Sam explained. "Let's start walking toward the red dot."

They moved slowly in a tight group toward the tree house, their eyes fixed on the phone in Sam's hand. They stopped right below the tree house.

"See?" Sam said. "The two dots are

right on top of each other. That means the treasure is here."

"Where?" Little John asked.

"I'm telling you, there's no treasure inside our tree house," Margaret said.

"I don't know what the treasure box looks like, but it could be in there and you might not know it," Sam said. "It could be a big metal box like this." He spread his hands wide apart. "Or it could be a tiny container like this." He held his thumb and first finger an inch apart. "It's probably more likely to be a tiny container."

Kaz hovered near the top of Claire's water bottle. "Claire!" he called. "I saw a metal box inside that tree branch. You wouldn't be able to get to it from the tree house unless you could pass through the branch. But there must be a hole in the tree down here somewhere. That's where the box is. I could feel air coming in from the Outside all around the box."

"Maybe there's a hole in the tree," Claire said to the others. "Maybe that's where the treasure is."

"There is a hole," Sam said. "It's over here." He led everyone around the tree.

Olivia shined her flashlight on a hole about the size of Claire's water bottle.

"There isn't anything inside it, though." Sam stuck his hand inside the hole.

Claire walked over. "Maybe you're not reaching in far enough," she said.

Sam stepped aside, and Claire put her whole arm inside the hole.

"Be careful, Claire," Olivia said nervously. "What if there's a bobcat or something in there, and it bites your arm off?"

"That hole isn't big enough for a bobcat," Kenya said.

"There's something in here," Claire said. With her cheek pressed against the tree trunk, she reached a little farther.

"Is it alive?" Olivia asked.

"No," Claire said. She rose up onto her tiptoes and wiggled her arm around some more. Finally, she pulled out a square metal box. "Is this your treasure?" she asked Sam.

"Maybe," he said. He took the box from her and opened it up.

"I want to see! I want to see!" Little John said, stretching his neck. But again, the ghosts didn't have a very good view from inside the water bottle.

Olivia shined her flashlight inside the metal box, and Sam pulled out a piece of paper. He unfolded it and read it under the light: "Congratulations! This paper proves that you are worthy of joining the Morgan Woods Treasure Club. Put the box back where you found it, and bring this paper to Daniel, Austin, or Hong. Welcome to the club." Sam punched his fist into the air. "Yes! I'm in."

"Congratulations," Kenya said flatly. "Now maybe you'll stay away from our tree house."

"How did you know the combination to get inside our tree house, anyway?" Margaret asked.

"Your brother," Sam admitted. "I told him that if he'd give me the combination so I could search inside for the treasure, I'd try to get him into the club."

"So are you the one who slammed the

door and told us to go awaaaaaay the other day, too?" Olivia asked.

"Yes," Sam said. "I was trying to get you to leave so I could look for the treasure."

"I told you guys it wasn't a real ghost," Kenya said.

* * * * * * * * * * * * * * * *

The next morning, Claire carried Kaz, Little John, Mom, and Pops back to the library inside her water bottle.

"Wait till you see the library," Kaz said to his parents. "You'll like it there. You'll see that it's the perfect new haunt for our family." He was excited to show his parents around the library, but a little nervous, too. What if they *didn't* like it? What if they didn't think it was the perfect new haunt for their family?

"We'll see," Mom said cautiously.

Claire skipped up the steps and opened her front door. "Hello? Mom, Dad, Grandma, I'm home!" she called as she closed the door behind her.

The ghosts passed through the side of the water bottle and expanded.

"Beckett? Cosmo? We're home, too," Kaz called out. "And guess who we brought with us!"

Cosmo poked his head out of the library craft room. "Woof! Woof!" he barked when he saw who was there.

"Cosmo!" Mom and Pops cried as Cosmo dog-paddled toward them. "It's so good to see you again!"

They both hugged the dog at the same time. Cosmo wagged his tail.

Then Beckett wafted in from the craft room. "Oh," he said when he saw them. "It's you."

Mom let go of Cosmo when she saw Beckett. Her mouth fell open, but she didn't say anything.

"Do you two know each other?" Kaz asked.

"You could say that . . . ," Beckett replied.

"How?" Little John asked.

"Yes, how?" Pops asked.

Mom smiled awkwardly. "I think that's a story for another day," she said. She wafted over to Beckett and held out her hand. "Good to see you again, Beckett," she said.

"Hmph," Beckett said as he shook her hand.

9//7